Arthur and the World Record

A Marc Brown ARTHUR Chapter Book

Arthur and the World Record

Text by Stephen Krensky

Based on a teleplay by Gerard Lewis

LITTLE, BROWN AND COMPANY

New York ∽ Boston

Little, Brown and Company

Time Warner Book Group
1271 Avenue of the Americas, New York, NY 10020
Visit our Web site at www.lb-kids.com

First Edition: April 2005

Text has been reviewed and assigned a reading level by Laurel S. Ernst,
M.A., Teachers College, Columbia University, New York, New York;
reading specialist, Chappaqua, New York.

Library of Congress Cataloging-in-Publication Data

Krensky, Stephen.
Arthur and the world record / text by Stephen Krensky ; based on
a teleplay by Gerard Lewis. — 1st ed.
p.   cm. — (A Marc Brown Arthur chapter book ; 33)
Summary: Arthur and his friends set out to make the world's largest
pizza so that their feat can be recorded in "The Book of Incredible
and Amazing World Records."
ISBN 0-316-12949-6 (hc) / ISBN 0-316-12681-0 (pb)
[1. World records — Fiction.   2. Pizza Fiction.   3. Aardvark — Fiction.
4. Animals — Fiction.]   I. Title.   II. Series: Brown, Marc Tolon. Marc
Brown Arthur chapter book ; 33.
PZ7.K883Atc 2004 [Fic] — dc22
2004004709

10 9 8 7 6 5 4 3

PHX (hc)

COM-MO (pb)

Printed in the United States of America

With love for Skye

Chapter 1

· · · · · · · · · · ·

Arthur and his friends were all sitting around the tree house. Binky and Buster looked bored. Francine and Muffy looked even more bored. The Brain would have looked bored, too, but he was trying hard not to look like everyone else.

"Listen to this!" said Arthur. He was holding *The Book of Incredible and Amazing World Records* in his lap. "I've read the whole thing. People have done the most amazing stuff. And a lot of them are ordinary people just like us. If we tried, I think we could make a world record ourselves."

"Wow!" said Buster. "We'd go down in history."

"Would they take pictures?" asked Muffy. "I'll need a new outfit for making history."

"What kind of record are you talking about?" asked the Brain.

Arthur flipped through the pages. "It could be anything. There's one in here about the world's tallest man. He was eight feet, eleven inches."

"Whoa!" said Binky. "That's twice as tall as I am."

Arthur kept reading. "And there's a guy who grew a beard more than seventeen feet long."

"Where did he put it?" asked Francine.

Arthur didn't know. "And there's even a guy who tried to walk backward all the way around the world."

"That could be quite a trip," said Buster.

Arthur turned to another section. "Think

about Thomas Edison. He has the record for patenting the most inventions. More than a thousand."

The Brain's mouth dropped open. "So many? If I'm going to break that one, I'd better get going."

He got up and left.

"Anyway," said Arthur, "I was thinking that we could break a world record together and make Elwood City famous."

Binky stood up. "I'd rather break a world record on my own. I just have to figure out which one."

He got up and left, too.

"I want my name in that book," said Muffy. "Just think of the fame and the glamour. I'm going to break the world record for . . . not talking."

"Not talking?" said Francine. "You?"

Muffy raised her eyebrows. "I might talk a lot, but I can stop any time I want. Even long enough to —"

She stopped, waved good-bye, and left.

"I guess if she's alone," said Francine, "she won't be tempted to speak." She frowned. "I wonder what would be best for me. Maybe something with soccer. . . . What if I kicked a ball in the air more times in a row than anyone else?"

"I don't know if that's in here," said Arthur.

"Well, if it's not, it should be." Francine stood up. "I'd better go practice."

So she left, too.

Buster rubbed his chin. "Growing a long beard would take forever." He stopped to think. "But I could break that record for walking backward. I'll see you later."

He went down the ladder.

Arthur looked around the tree house. He was all alone. "Maybe I could get the record for emptying a tree house faster than ever before."

Chapter 2

Arthur was sitting on the floor of his room.

"Careful . . . careful . . . ," he said to himself. He placed another playing card down on a pile growing in front of him.

Pal was watching. He wagged his tail.

"Gently, Pal," said Arthur. "I'm building a house of cards. It's very delicate. If your tail hits the floor too hard, the vibrations could knock it over."

Pal cocked his head at the cards.

"Some people just build straight up," Arthur went on, "trying to see how high they can go. I like starting with a broader base and building up gradually."

He added another one.

"Look, Pal. Seventy-nine cards down. Only twelve thousand more to break the world record." He stretched his arms. "We could be here a while."

Arthur stepped out of a revolving door outside the lobby of a giant skyscraper. The walls on either side were not made of steel or stone. They were made all out of cards.

"Look, there he is!" said a news photographer. Several others also raised their cameras and started taking pictures.

Arthur raised one arm to shield his eyes from the bright flashes.

A man in the crowd held up a little boy and pointed at Arthur.

"See that boy, son? That's Arthur Read. He's the one who designed and built Arthur

Towers. They're calling it one of the Eight Wonders of the World."

"I thought there were only Seven Wonders in the World," said the man next to him.

"There were," the first man explained, "until Arthur Towers appeared."

Arthur allowed himself a smile as he stepped to a waiting limousine. A lot of people had laughed when he first proposed his project. But he had stood firm, and he had followed through. And the fruits of his labor now towered over the city for everyone to admire.

A uniformed chauffeur opened his limousine door. Arthur turned back for a last picture. At that moment, he spotted D.W. coming out another door in the building. She gripped the doorknob firmly — and then slammed the door shut behind her.

"Noooooooo!" cried Arthur.

The skyscraper teetered eerily.

"Run!" cried one onlooker.

"Run for your lives!" shouted another.
Arthur glared at his sister.
"Oops!" said D.W.

Arthur blinked. He was up to the fourth floor on his house of cards. So far so good, but it was better to be safe, he thought. He stood up and walked over to his door.

D.W. was playing in her room across the hall.

"D.W.," he said, "you're not allowed to come in my room today. I'm working on an important project."

She stood up. "You don't have to be so bossy. I don't want to go in your room, anyway. I have much better things to do."

She walked over and slammed her door shut.

Arthur winced. Then he heard a fluttering noise behind him. He turned around to see his house of cards collapsing to the floor.

Pal padded over and sniffed the remains. He let out a little whine.

Arthur sighed. "I know just how you feel," he said.

Chapter 3

. . . .

Francine and Muffy were out working on their own records. Although they were not working together, they were keeping each other company.

"One hundred and eight . . . one hundred and nine . . . one hundred and ten . . . ," counted Francine as she slowly moved down the street. She couldn't move very quickly because she was bouncing a soccer ball off her foot. "As long as I keep it from hitting the ground, I'm all set."

Muffy nodded. She gave Francine a big thumbs-up.

"Thanks," said Francine. "If I keep

this up, I could break the world record today."

Muffy nodded again.

"Wow!" said Francine. "You're pretty good, Muffy. You haven't talked in two hours. It must be driving you crazy."

Muffy rolled her eyes.

"I can imagine," said Francine. "Let's see . . . Where am I? One hundred and nineteen . . . one hundred and twenty . . ."

She was concentrating hard on the ball, and so was Muffy. Neither of them saw Buster coming the other way.

Buster didn't see them, either. He was walking backward down the sidewalk with halting little steps. He was also wearing a harness over his shoulders. It held up two rearview mirrors so that Buster could see where he was going. Unfortunately, he was still learning how to use them.

As the three of them met at the corner, their shadows collided first.

"Hey!" cried Francine. But before she could move aside, her foot hit the back of Buster's knee.

"Ouch!" said Buster.

Francine's ball bounced off his back and skittered away.

"Oh, no!" She sighed.

"Watch where you're going, Buster!" Muffy snapped. "We're doing important stuff here."

"I'm doing the best I can," he said. "But walking backward is trickier than it looks."

"I don't care how tricky it is," said Muffy. "You shouldn't be —" Suddenly, she clapped her hand over her mouth. "I spoke! How could I do that? I can't believe it! Now I have to start over. That's two hours down the drain."

Francine ran over to pick up her ball. "Tell me about it."

"Sorry," said Buster. "I'm still getting used to these rearview mirrors. Pretty neat, huh?"

He tried to use them to look both ways to cross the street. "Now I'm looking left . . . but actually I'm looking right . . . or is it the other way around? Wait! There is no other way around. Because then I'd be back where I started. Or would I?"

Buster scratched his head.

"Uh, excuse me," he said to the girls. "I've been going around and around on this block because I was a little nervous about crossing the street. I don't suppose you could help me look both ways. . . ."

"I suppose," said Francine.

"So, is it okay to cross now?" Buster asked.

"All clear," said Muffy.

"Great. See you later. And good luck with your records."

"Thanks," said Francine. "And Buster, whether you break the record or not . . ."

"Yes?" he said.

Francine smiled. "We hope you survive the day."

Chapter 4

"Survive the day?" Buster repeated these words to himself as he continued his shuffling steps. What had Francine meant by that? What was so special about the day? Why wouldn't he survive it?

"Hey, watch it, buddy!"

"Look where you're going!"

"Wake up, Mirror Boy!"

All of these remarks were aimed at Buster, because he kept bumping into people on the sidewalk. But he was so busy trying to figure out what Francine had meant that he barely noticed them.

"Excuse me. . . . Coming through. . . . World record in progress. . . ."

It wasn't just walking backward, though, that required his attention. His mirrors needed constant adjustment. He was fiddling with them near Binky's house when he noticed something.

Binky was sitting at a picnic table in his backyard. Actually, he wasn't really sitting. He was more like slumping. It was not a position Buster had ever seen Binky in before.

"Oooooooooooh!" Binky groaned, clutching his stomach.

Buster shuffled over for a closer look. On the table was a half-built Popsicle stick bridge. Next to it were some melting Popsicles and a pile of wrappers.

"Hey, Binky!"

He heard another groan.

"Binky, it's me, Buster."

"I know who it is," said Binky, without moving.

"Are you all right?"

Binky raised his head. "I will be — someday. Someday in the distant future." He blinked at Buster. "What's all that stuff you're wearing?"

Buster smiled. "I'm walking backward to break the world record. The mirrors help me see where I'm going. Sort of."

"I wish I'd thought of doing that," said Binky. "It would have been less painful."

Buster looked at the table. "What are you making?" he asked.

Binky groaned. "I was building the world's largest Popsicle stick bridge. It was going to be big — really big. But, of course, I needed the right supplies. At first it wasn't so bad. But now I feel sick. I must have eaten twenty-five Popsicles."

"Why did you do that?" asked Buster.

Binky made a face. "How else was I going to get the Popsicle sticks?"

"Oh," said Buster, "You know, my mom

21

once made a Popsicle stick lampshade out of four hundred Popsicle sticks."

"Four hundred!" said Binky. "Wow! She must have a stomach of steel."

Buster shook his head. "No. She just bought her sticks at the craft shop."

Binky rubbed his stomach. "You mean I ate all those Popsicles for nothing?"

"Oh, I wouldn't say that. You could make the world's biggest Popsicle stick bridge and set the record for eating the most Popsicles, too." He paused. "That would probably get you mentioned on two different pages."

Binky sighed. "Maybe three — if I also got the record for being the most sick." He put his head back down on the table.

Buster hadn't thought of that. "That would be very impressive."

Binky may have agreed with him, but all Buster heard was the biggest groan yet.

Chapter 5

● ● ● ● ● ● ● ● ● ● ●

Arthur was sitting in his yard taking deep breaths. Four paper cups were lined up in front of him.

Arthur stared at them.

"Well, here they are," he said.

Of course, the cups said nothing. One of them, however, might have moved a little.

"Maybe it's important to line them up perfectly," Arthur added.

He nudged one of the cups slightly forward.

"That's better."

The cups still said nothing.

"Oh, well," said Arthur. "I don't suppose it will help to delay this any longer. I guess the time has come."

He picked up one cup and raised it toward his mouth — and then stopped.

The worm in the cup was wriggling over the side.

Arthur made a face.

"Yuck!" said Muffy, coming up behind him.

Francine was there, too. "You aren't really going to eat that, are you?" she asked.

Arthur put down the cup. "Well," he said, "I was trying to decide if I should be practicing."

"Practicing what?" asked Muffy. "Eating bugs?"

"Not bugs, worms." Arthur shuddered. "Not that I'm sure it makes much of a difference. But somebody ate sixty of these in less than a minute."

"Sixty!" said Francine. She placed her hand on her stomach. "I could never be that hungry."

Muffy nodded. "Even if they were served in the finest restaurant. But we do still want to get into the book."

"Can you find us some other record to break?" Francine asked. "Kicking a soccer ball is too boring."

"And giving up talking isn't good, either," said Muffy. "I have too much to say."

Arthur flipped through the pages. "There are lots of things in here. Let's see . . . Here's a guy who once had a hundred bees in his mouth for ten seconds."

"Too dangerous," said Francine.

"Another guy got into a bathtub with forty rattlesnakes."

"Those are disgusting," said Muffy. "Aren't there any records more . . . glamorous? What about the world's biggest bubble bath? Or shopping spree?"

"No . . . I don't see anything like that. But if you want glamorous, there was a woman who had fingernails ten feet long."

"Hmmmmm," said Muffy. "That sounds interesting."

"Unfortunately," said Arthur, "it says here that fingernails only grow at the rate of three inches a year. So you'd have to wait almost forty years."

Muffy frowned. "Not to mention all the time I'd spend putting on nail polish."

"Find something else," said Francine. "Something where if we make a mistake, we don't have to start over from scratch."

"Hey! Here's a record." Arthur pointed at the page. "The world's largest pizza. It was thirty feet wide. That's big, but not so big we couldn't make one bigger. How long could that take?"

Muffy and Francine looked at each other.

"I could talk while we were making it, couldn't I?" Muffy asked.

"Of course," said Francine. "And I wouldn't have to bounce any toppings off my foot, would I?"

"Certainly not," said Muffy.

They both turned back to Arthur.

"Okay!" they said together.

Chapter 6

• • • • • • • • • • • •

Arthur, Binky, Francine, and Muffy came running up to the Brain outside his house. Buster was with them, too, but he was a little bit behind because he was still walking backward.

"Guess what, Brain?" said Arthur. "We have —"

The Brain held up a hand. "Hold on, Arthur. I'm glad all of you are here. You will make excellent witnesses."

"Witnesses?" said Francine. "Witnesses to what?"

"To history!" said the Brain. "I'm just about ready to demonstrate."

He took a screwdriver and made a few last adjustments.

"There! It's all set."

"What is it?" asked Binky.

The Brain smiled proudly. "A remote-control flying lawn sprinkler. The first in the world, I believe."

"It looks like an airplane with a garden hose attached," said Francine.

"To the layman, maybe," said the Brain. "Actually, it is a complicated matrix of aerodynamic and hydraulic interfaces. Now stand back."

The Brain punched a few buttons. The airplane took off.

"Stage One complete. Now for Stage Two." The Brain turned a dial.

As the airplane banked around, spray was released from the garden hose. It sprinkled over the ground.

"You see!" he said. "It's working."

"Yes, but . . . ," said Arthur.

"History in the making!" the Brain went on. "Aren't you glad you were here?"

"Yes, but . . . ," said Francine.

"Duck!" cried Muffy.

The plane buzzed over their heads, soaking them thoroughly.

"That shouldn't have happened," said the Brain, punching one button after another.

"Uh-oh!" said Buster, who had just arrived.

The plane had stalled in midair. It sputtered once — and then crashed to the ground.

"Sorry," said the Brain. "I guess I haven't worked out all the details yet. Apparently, the global positioning navigator still needs work."

"I'm sure you'll figure it out," said Arthur. "But we were wondering if you'd like to join us."

"We're thinking of making the world's largest pizza," said Muffy.

"With your help," said Francine.

The Brain scratched his head. He looked down at his flying sprinkler.

"Hmmm . . . the world's largest pizza, eh? I'll bet Edison never thought of that."

"So let's work on the details," said Arthur.

It took about an hour for everything to be decided.

"All right," said Arthur. "It looks like we'll need five hundred pounds of flour, one hundred pounds of cheese, and twenty-five gallons of tomato sauce. Muffy, you're in charge of getting donations. That many ingredients are going to be expensive."

"Right. I'll start with my dad."

"Binky and I will make the rack to cook the pizza on," said the Brain. "The playing field at school will probably be the safest open space."

"We'll need permission from Mr. Haney," said Francine. "I'll take care of that."

"And I'll ask my dad to get the tin foil and the barbecue coals," said Arthur. "Buster?"

"Right here."

"It's hard to tell if you're listening since you're not looking at me."

"I can see you in the mirror."

"Okay. Since your mom's a reporter, you're in charge of contacting the newspapers and TV stations."

Buster nodded — which shook his mirrors loose again.

"All right," said Arthur, "I think that covers everything."

"Don't worry," said Binky. "This whole thing will be a piece of cake."

Everyone stared at him.

"Hey," said Binky, "you know what I mean."

Chapter 7

• • • • • • • • • • • •

At dinner the next night, Arthur brought his family up to date.

"Everything seems to be coming along," he said. "Francine took care of all the permissions, and Buster's mom has contacted the TV stations. We want to make sure we have plenty of proof for the book people."

Arthur entered a long, dark chamber all alone. At the far end, three figures in black robes sat behind a high bench.

"Step forward, Mr. Read," said the one in the middle. "We understand you wish to be

included in the next edition of The Book of Incredible and Amazing World Records.*"

Arthur swallowed nervously. "That's right, Your Honors. I have photographs and video-tapes and signatures of everyone who helped."

"And you call that proof?" said the figure on the right.

"I was hoping it would be enough," said Arthur.

"We'll be the judges of that," said the figure on the left.

"Arthur?" said Dad.

"Huh?"

"What about food?"

"Oh, Muffy and her dad got in touch with the supermarket. Everything we need has been ordered. And they'll keep it re-frigerated until we pick it up."

"Won't cooking a pizza that big be tricky?" Mom asked.

Arthur nodded. "That's why we put the Brain in charge of making the calculations. He started to explain it to me — something about BTUs, I think. He also worked out a formula for how much charcoal we need per square foot. As long as he understands it, that's all that matters."

"Well, whatever happens," said Mom, "the part I like best is that you're all working together."

Arthur nodded. "Buster's still trying to break his own record, though. He even turned around his desk at school so that he wouldn't accidentally stand up and walk forward by mistake."

"Really?" said Dad. "What did Mr. Ratburn say about that?"

"He's decided to consider it a kind of science experiment. He also said that anything that helps Buster concentrate might be an improvement."

Dad nodded. "Sounds like you have everything covered."

"Not everything," said D.W.

"What do you mean?" asked Arthur.

"What if the pizza gets stolen?" she asked.

"Stolen?" Arthur frowned. "How?"

"Well," said D.W., "with all that cheese . . . an army of mice might sneak up and carry it off."

Arthur rolled his eyes. "That won't happen, D.W."

"But if it did, how would you stop it?"

"MOM!"

Mrs. Read stopped to think. "D.W.," she said after a moment, "what are mice afraid of?"

"Cats."

"So maybe you could make pictures of cats we could put up to scare away the mice."

D.W. nodded. "I could do that."

"Of course," said Dad, "even without armies of mice, there are plenty of other things to plan for. Whenever you cook on a big scale, there are always surprises."

"I know," said Arthur. "I just hope we're ready for them."

Chapter 8

• • • • • • • • • • •

The soccer field at Lakewood Elementary was a busy place that Saturday morning. Everyone had gathered for the big event, and hopes were running high.

At least they had begun that way. The food preparations had started early with Francine and Muffy mixing pizza dough. As time had passed, they both had become covered in flour. At this point they looked like two out-of-season snowmen.

Nearby, Binky was spinning the dough to thin it out. He had never tried this before, but he had seen it done on TV. At

first, most of his throws had landed in the tree branches. But he was getting better.

The dough that survived had been passed on to Mr. Read, who connected each piece to a growing carpet of dough.

"My arms are going to fall off, they're so tired," said Francine.

"No stopping now," said Arthur. "There's still too much to do."

Muffy rubbed flour off her nose. "We've been at this for hours. I'm starting to think it's impossible."

"Maybe we bit off more than we can chew," said Binky, pulling some dough out of his hair.

"Time for a break," said Francine.

"You can't take a break," Arthur insisted. He looked at his clipboard. "We're already an hour behind schedule. Buster should be here soon," said Arthur. "You can rest when he takes your place."

"But I'm exhausted now," said Muffy. "My hands are so pooped, even my fingernails are tired."

"We'll be back soon," said Francine. "We promise."

"You promise?" Arthur gaped at them. *"The Book of Incredible and Amazing World Records* doesn't care about promises. It isn't interested in good intentions. It only cares about results."

"I never thought about it that way," said Binky. He yawned. "I think I'll take five, too."

Arthur shook his head as Binky, Francine, and Muffy walked away. "This is terrible! We're going to get into the *Book of World Records* as the biggest flop in history. I'll be humiliated."

"All right, class," said Mr. Ratburn, "it's time to discuss the greatest fiascos in history. We're

talking about the disasters that no one ever forgets. Yes, Muffy?"

"I was watching this awards show on TV last year. There was this one actress whose outfit was really ridiculous."

"A sad day for fashion, I'm sure," said Mr. Ratburn. "But not a significant moment in the larger historical record."

Francine raised her hand. "What about the Titanic?"

Mr. Ratburn nodded. "That's certainly one. Significant and tragic. A night to remember. Any others?"

The Brain had one. "Napoleon's defeat at Waterloo?"

"Excellent," said Mr. Ratburn. "Not his best day by a long shot. Definitely on anyone's Top Ten list. Let's see, though . . . What about the worst one of all? The flop that stands head and shoulders above the rest. Any ideas?"

Almost every hand in the class went up.

"My, my," said Mr. Ratburn. "You all seem very positive about this. Perhaps we could all say it together."

"ARTHUR'S PIZZA!" cried the whole class.

Chapter 9

• • • • • • • • • • • •

Arthur sat at the edge of the soccer field, his head in his hands. What a terrible day! Why had he ever gotten himself into this mess? What had made him think something like this could really happen?

"I wish I could just disappear," he murmured. He knew that his father and the Brain were still working, but every second put them further and further behind.

"We're not going to be able do it," he said. "This was the dumbest idea I ever had. I should —"

"Hey!" said the Brain. "Here comes Buster."

Arthur sighed. "Oh, great. Better late than never, I suppose. But he's just one person. And what difference can one —"

Arthur stopped speaking because he had looked up. It was true that Buster was coming — and still walking backward — but he wasn't alone. A crowd was following him, including Arthur's mom, Grandma Thora, Mr. Ratburn, Sue Ellen, Fern, and many others.

The Brain smiled. "I think he brought half the town with him."

"Hi, Arthur!" said Buster, waving. "Look who I found."

Before Arthur could fully absorb this, he heard his name called from the other end of the field.

"Yoo hoo! Arthur!"

It was Francine and Muffy. But they weren't alone, either. The other half of the town seemed to be with them. Muffy's

dad was there, and the mechanics from his auto dealership. And Prunella, Catherine, and the Brain's mom.

"For an industrial-sized pizza you need industrial-strength equipment," she said. "So I brought my mixing machines from the ice cream shop."

Arthur was amazed. "This is great!"

Everyone got busy. Several people unrolled long rolls of chicken wire over the hot coals that the Brain had prepared. Arthur's father stirred the tomato sauce. Francine and Muffy went back to mixing dough, but this time they had help.

When Mr. Read thought the carpet of dough was big enough, it was unrolled over the chicken wire. Then he cut the edge to make it round.

"But how are we going to get the tomato sauce over the middle?" asked Arthur.

"It's too far to reach, and we can't walk over the rest of the dough to get there."

"Have no fear," said the Brain. "We've got that covered, so to speak."

He took out his remote control lawn sprinkler. It was now connected to a vat of tomato sauce. The airplane whizzed back and forth, depositing the sauce over everything except the crowd of people.

Then the cheese went on, clumped loosely into balls, and launched by an army of spatulas.

"Can someone hit that bare spot in the middle?" asked Mr. Read. "Oh, good shot, Francine!"

Slices of pepperoni came next, followed by olives.

"No juggling the olives," Muffy told Binky. "You're not supposed to play with your food."

Arthur stepped way back to take everything in.

"So what do you think?" his mom asked him.

"Well," said Arthur, beaming, "this just may work, after all."

Chapter 10

. . . .

"Is it time yet?"

This was the question everyone had been asking. Arthur must have said "no" fifty times, but now he didn't.

"The biggest pizza in the world is now ready to eat!" he announced.

"You do the cutting," said his father. "It was your idea, don't forget."

"I won't," said Arthur, smiling. He cut off a piece and handed it to Buster. Then the Brain, Francine, Muffy, and Binky came forward to pose for pictures.

Everyone cheered. "Speech, Arthur! Speech!" they cried.

Arthur turned a little red as he stepped forward. "Wow, guys! I don't really know what to say, so I'm going to keep this short. Thanks for helping out and making all this possible. We did it! Elwood City has made the biggest pizza in the world. The record belongs to us all. And now, EVERYBODY EAT!"

He didn't have to ask twice. As everybody dug in, Buster pulled Arthur aside. "Do you remember," he asked, "how far I have to walk to break the record for walking backward?"

"I think it was about eight thousand miles."

Buster nodded. "Oh. Then I'm going to need my strength."

He stepped forward toward the pizza.

"Uh-oh," said Arthur. "Um, Buster . . ."

"What?"

"Do you realize what you just did?"

Buster blinked. "Oh, no! I just walked forward." He sighed deeply. "I guess I'll have to start over."

And taking an extra slice with him, he slowly backed away.